Game Boy

Reloaded

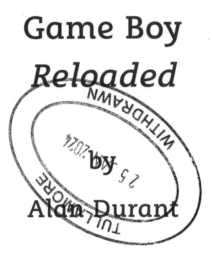

by

Alan Durant

Illustrated by Sue Mason

You do not need to read this page – just get on with the book!

First published in 2005 in Great Britain by
Barrington Stoke Ltd
18 Walker St, Edinburgh, EH3 7LP

www.barringtonstoke.co.uk

This edition published in 2007

ISBN 978-1-84299-566-2

Printed in Great Britain by Bell & Bain Ltd

Meet The Author – Alan Durant

Who is your favourite football player?
My son Kit
How tall are you?
4 cm and a half
What's your favourite smell?
Petrol
Can you do a one-handed press-up?
No, but I can hop
What is your first memory?
I've forgotten
Do you have a best friend?
My mum quite likes me

Meet The Illustrator – Sue Mason

What is your favourite cheese?
Stinking Bishop
How big are your feet?
Size 5 ... with toes like small prawns
What colour is your mobile phone?
Scuffed silver
Which do you prefer: gnomes or pixies?
Definitely pixies
What is your nickname?
Spu Basin
What's your best book?
Anything by the author Alan Durant

For my nephew Max Lyon – and for my
daughter Josie, who gave me
the title
A.D.

For Mum and Dad
with huge love
xx
S.M.

Contents

Level 1

"Come away from there, Zak!" Mia shouted.

Mia often shouted at Zak. He was her little brother and he was a pest. He was always doing things he shouldn't. Just now he was throwing stones into the canal. That was OK. But he was standing too near the water. He might fall in – and then they'd both be in trouble.

Mum had told Mia to look after Zak.

"He's old enough to look after himself," Mia had grumbled.

But Mum didn't think so. So here Mia was, looking after her little brother yet again. She wanted to be in her room, playing Planet Quest on her GameBoy. It wasn't fair.

"Zak, don't be stupid! Get away from there!" Mia shouted once more.

Zak took no notice. He never did. Mia marched up to him, huffing with anger.

"Look, Mia," Zak said. He pointed at something floating in the water. "Look at that."

But she was too cross to look. "It's just a bit of old rubbish," she said and she pulled Zak back. The canal was full of rubbish. "Now come away. It's all muddy here."

But Zak wouldn't come. "No, look," he said again. "It looks like a GameBoy game. Over there, in the water."

This time Mia did look. She loved her GameBoy. So did Zak – but she never let him play it. He took it sometimes when she wasn't around, and he never put it back. It drove her mad.

"I'm going to get it," Zak said.

"No, stay here," said Mia. "You'll only get wet. I'll try."

Mia found a long stick. She reached out into the water to pull the floating thing in. She thought it would be hard but it was easy. It was almost as if she didn't need the stick. The thing seemed to bob towards her on its own. It was a small, grey cartridge. Zak was right – it was a GameBoy game!

Mia was excited as she picked the game out of the water. Zak was excited, too. He ran over. "Let's see, let's see!" he shouted.

Mia held it away from him. She shook the water off it. "It's mine," she said.

"I saw it first!" he complained.

"But I got it out," Mia said.

They looked at the game together. It had no picture or name on it. But there was a line of print. Mia rubbed the game dry on her coat.

"Warning! This experience may seriously damage your health," she read aloud. She frowned. "Weird," she said.

"Cool," said Zak. "I wonder what game it is."

Mia gave a shrug. "I don't think it'll work anyway," she said. "The water will have ruined it."

"Let's try it," said Zak.

"*I* will," said Mia, "as soon as we get home."

She put the game in her coat pocket.

Suddenly Zak put his hand on Mia's arm. "Somebody's watching us," he whispered, with a shiver. "Look on the bridge."

Mia gave a sigh. Zak was always imagining things. But when she looked, she saw that Zak was right again. There *was* a man standing on the bridge over the canal. He was staring at them. He looked strange. He was bald, except for a small cone of white hair on top of his head. He wore thick glasses which made his eyes look huge. His eyes had an odd gleam to them as well. He smiled at Mia, showing a row of silver-capped teeth.

Now Mia shivered too. "Let's go," she said. She grabbed Zak's hand and they ran away.

Level 2

Mia wanted to try out the game as soon as she got home. She went to her room and took her GameBoy down from the shelf. She loaded the new game. Would it work after it had got wet? But she didn't get the chance to find out because her mum called her, just as she was about to turn on her GameBoy.

She dropped it on her bed and went downstairs.

It was nearly half an hour later when at last Mia could go back upstairs. Her mum had wanted to check her spelling homework and then Mia had to set the table for lunch. When, at last, she was back in her room, she was really angry to see that the GameBoy and her new game had gone.

"Zak!" she hissed. "Just wait till I get my hands on him! I'll kill the little pest ...!"

Mia stomped into Zak's room. Yes, the GameBoy was there all right, just as she'd suspected. It was lying on Zak's bed. But there was no sign at all of her little brother. He *had* been playing the game. The GameBoy was still on and it felt warm.

Mia looked at the screen. There was an underwater scene with seaweed and fish. Well, at least the game worked. That was good. She sat down on Zak's bed and pushed her thumbs down on the controls. It looked as if this was one of those games where there was no person to move about. It was as if everything was happening to you, the player. She'd played plenty of games like that before.

She moved her left thumb over the cross direction controls, while pressing the A button so that she weaved in and out of the plants. Should she catch or dodge the fish that came onto the screen now and then? She decided to play safe and dodge them for the moment.

She moved faster as she got used to the game. Now she was racing across the sea floor. She jumped over any rocks that blocked her way. It was easy and fun. There weren't any dangers, just a few obstacles. That's how it seemed anyway.

But then she saw the jellyfish.

They were falling through the water ahead of her like purple parachutes. Mia knew she had to dodge them. Jellyfish stung. If she bumped into one of them, they would take away some of her power. They might kill her. She didn't know how poisonous the jellyfish were. She didn't want to find out.

She waited till the first lot of jellyfish had dropped and vanished. Then she sprinted as fast as she could. She froze when the next lot of jellyfish fell, then dodged them too. One nearly got her, but she took a step back just in time.

At last, she was past the jellyfish. She saw in the sea ahead of her some kind of wreck. Perhaps it was an old ship, full of treasure ... that would be cool.

She was really into the game now. She could feel the cold water against her skin. She could taste its saltiness. She could see ... a boy! He was standing on the old

ship, waving at her. She stopped, amazed, confused.

It was Zak ... and behind him ... was a giant octopus! Its tentacles were reaching out towards Zak.

Mia tried to shout a warning, but her cry was lost in bubbles.

The tentacles closed around Zak.

There was nothing Mia could do.

An instant later, Zak and the octopus vanished into the wreck.

Level 3

Mia was in shock.

For a start, she'd just seen her little brother inside the game she was playing.

Then she'd seen him grabbed by a giant octopus.

But most shocking of all, Mia knew suddenly that she wasn't lying on Zak's bed playing her GameBoy any more. Now she was part of the game. She was playing it from the inside! She was really under the sea! The wreck was really there in front of her.

She shut her eyes, shook her head, but nothing changed. She was still underwater. Only this wasn't like being underwater in real life. She could breathe like fish did. She could walk along the bottom of the sea, too. Somehow, she and Zak had been sucked into the game. It was incredible. No wonder the game had a health warning!

Mia didn't understand what had happened. But she knew what she had to do next – get inside the wreck and rescue her little brother. She'd wasted too much time already. The octopus could have crushed him by now.

She ran on till she got to the wreck. She looked for a place to enter – a door or a hole or something. Zak and the octopus had got in, so she must be able to.

At last she saw an opening. It was a jagged hole in the ship's side. If she jumped up and kicked her legs she should be able to get through.

Something moved in the water near her. She looked round quickly and gasped. It was a shark – a great white shark, with a mouth full of huge teeth. And it was heading for her!

There was no time to lose. She jumped and kicked hard and fast, and pushed up through the water with her arms. Would she reach the hole before the shark got her? She could see it out of the corner of her eye. It was racing towards her, its fin cutting through the water, its mouth open ready to snap.

She swam harder, stronger, kicked faster.

Now she was at the hole. Her head was through, her body was through. The shark was right behind her.

One last kick! Mia dragged her legs up and ... she was through – into the ship!

Everything went black.

Level 4

Mia gave a big sigh of relief. She'd made it – just. That had been too close.

When she looked down, she saw that the bottoms of her shoes were torn to shreds. If she'd been even a teeny bit slower, the shark would have got her – and then what? She'd have had to go back to the start of the game. Then how would she ever have found Zak?

She looked about her. If this was a game, then she must be on the next level now. There was no sign of Zak anywhere. There was nothing here at all at the bottom of the ship. She swam through another hole up to the next deck.

There wasn't much on this deck either – just some old ropes and a few rusty cannons. There was still no sign of Zak. She was going to carry on swimming upwards, but changed her mind. There were some small gold coins floating in the water around the deck. She thought perhaps she should collect them. You often had to collect things in GameBoy games. The coins might give her more power or energy.

Mia took a step to the left and grabbed a coin. She was surprised at how light it was. It was no heavier than a feather. She put it in her pocket and moved on. She collected a second coin and a third, fourth, fifth ... She was reaching to pick up another one when one of the wooden planks she was standing on started to crack.

"Ow!" she cried. Her left foot went straight through the floor. Now the plank under her right foot started to creak and crack. She pulled out her left foot and stepped away quickly. She would have to be more careful. Looking at the floor she could see that the wood was rotten and split in lots of places. It wasn't safe to walk across.

Her leg hurt. No wonder! There was a big splinter of wood in it. She'd had splinters before but never one as big as this. Just looking at it made her feel sick. She had to get it out. She got hold of the loose end of the splinter, shut her eyes and yanked.

"Ah!" Her shout of pain came out in a burst of bubbles. The splinter had come out.

There wasn't even a mark on her skin.

Weird, she thought. But then this was a weird game.

She decided not to pick up any more coins. Instead she swam up again.

The next deck up was empty, too. No, hold on a minute – there in the corner in the gloom was some kind of box. She went closer, stepping with care on the creaky planks.

It wasn't a box. It was a chest – a treasure chest! She saw something else, too. In front of the chest was a shoe. It was a small blue trainer and she knew at once it was Zak's. So he had been here! She was on the right track. But Zak wasn't there now. Had the octopus got him or had he got away? Mia needed to find out. But how? There didn't seem to be any way out from this deck.

Mia went about the deck with great care. She was looking for a hidden door or an escape hatch. No, there wasn't one. It had to be the chest then. The answer must be in there. She went towards it.

Mia was almost in front of the chest when something made her stop and look down. The planks on the floor didn't look right here. They were cracked, but the cracks had clean smooth edges and they made a perfect square. Mia bent down to look.

She rested her hand on the wooden square and pushed softly. Whomp! The wood dropped open. It was a trapdoor! Mia almost fell, but she stopped herself just in time. She moved back and one of the coins she'd picked up fell out of her pocket, into the gap where the trapdoor had been. She watched it spin through the dark, down and down, till it vanished. She listened but she didn't hear it land. She shivered. That could have been her.

Mia stepped around the hole in the floor with great care. Now she was in front of the chest. She touched it. It felt solid enough. She tried to lift the lid, but she couldn't make it move. There was no key, not even any lock, just a tiny slit in the front of the chest. She put her eye against the slit, but all she could see was blackness. She ran her hand over the chest. Perhaps there was a secret button that might open the lid? But she couldn't find one.

It was frustrating. She'd got this far and now she was stuck. Zak had got to the next level and so must she. She was a much better GameBoy player than he was, the little pest. *Think, Mia*, she said to herself. *If*

*you were at the controls now, how would
you solve this problem?*

She looked again at the tiny slit in the
chest. And then she knew. This wasn't a
treasure chest exactly – it was a giant
moneybox! Mia took one of the coins out of
her pocket and slipped it into the slit in the
chest. It was a perfect fit. The lid flew open.

Mia climbed in. The lid slammed shut
behind her.

Level 5

Mia was on an island. Behind her was the sea, in front of her, on a far-off hill, was an old castle. *That must be where she had to get to on this level*, she thought. Right in front of her were three paths. She had to choose which one to take. Mia sat down on a rock to think.

Mia put her hand in her pocket. She wanted to see if the gold coins were still there in this new level. They were – but there were only two left. Three had gone. She thought about this. One had dropped out, when she'd nearly fallen through the trapdoor and she'd used one to open the chest. What about the third one? She remembered the splinter and how her skin had suddenly got better. She must have lost a coin then. The coins were like lives. Well, it was good to know she still had two left to help her on this new level. She would need them, she was sure of that.

Mia looked hard at the three paths. Which one went to the castle? The one on the left was overgrown with bushes and she didn't like the look of it – anything could be hiding in there. The one on the right went down to the sea. Well, that was no good. To get to the castle she had to go up, not down. The middle one looked the best. It was straight and open. Yes, she'd take that one.

She'd wasted quite a lot of time already and the game might have a time limit, so she jogged down the path. She kept looking out for any dangers. Even so, she nearly trod on a small monkey that jumped down in front of her. An instant later another jumped down too, and then a third. They looked friendly, but she knew that meant nothing. In this game, you had to be ready for anything.

Perhaps she should turn back. But no, she'd chosen this path – she must carry on. She moved forward with slow, careful steps. There were lots more monkeys now, but they didn't show any interest in her as she walked among them. They reminded her a bit of Zak – only they were much sweeter.

Mia was so busy staring at the monkeys that she didn't see the loop of rope half-hidden in the earth on the ground in front of her. She stepped into it. The rope went tight

round her ankle. "Agh!" she yelled, as the rope yanked her ankle and then the rest of her body up through the air! Up and up she went, until she was hanging upside down by her ankle from a tree. But that wasn't the worst thing. The path had come to a deadly dead end. Now she was dangling over the edge of a cliff in some crazy bungee nightmare!

"Help!" she cried, but there was no point. Who could hear her? There was no one to rescue her. For once in her life she wished that Zak was around. The rope jerked and Mia twisted round to look up. The rope jerked again. Mia saw with panic that the branch the rope was tied round was breaking. Soon it would snap and she would fall onto the rocks far below.

She tried to swing herself to and fro to see if she could get near to the cliff edge and grip onto something. But all she did was jiggle another of the coins out of her pocket. It flipped past her.

"Damn!" she shouted. "Damn, damn, damn!"

Suddenly she felt a tug on her ankle. She was being pulled up again towards the tree.

"Hey," she shouted. What on earth was going on now?

As soon as she was close, she reached out and grabbed hold of a thick branch. It was hard work but bit-by-bit she dragged herself up and onto the branch. She pulled herself along the branch until at last she was safely above the path again. At once, the rope vanished. She took a deep breath. *That's it*, she thought, *another life gone*. Only one more left.

She'd chosen the wrong path. She should have known. The simple choice wouldn't be the right one. Nothing in this game was that easy. She went back and tried the overgrown path, but that one soon came to a dead end too. It had to be the third path then – the one that went down to the sea. She started off down it.

The path went down and then up, down and up, this way and that. There were things in the way too – fallen trees she had to climb or jump over and small tunnels Mia had to crawl through. It was hard work and her legs hurt by the time she could see the castle again. Normally, when she played her GameBoy game all that hurt was her thumbs. This was something else!

Mia stood still for a few moments, panting, as she stared at the castle. It was impressive. It was huge. It had a drawbridge entrance and high walls. At the very top was a magnificent tower in the shape of a skull. A flag flapped in the wind – it was the skull and crossbones. This was a pirate castle! Mia could see something else, too. There was someone in the tower. A tiny figure was leaning out of one of the eye-windows of the skull tower and waving madly. Even from so far away, Mia knew who it was – Zak! It looked as if he was trapped in the tower.

"Zak!" she shouted. "Zak! I'm coming."

She ran with new energy along the path to the castle, crossed the drawbridge and raced inside.

Everything went black.

Level 6

A warning flashed in the darkness –

Beware! You have entered the Castle of Redbeard, the Pirate King. Your life is in danger. Many enter, but few depart. Do you dare continue?

Mia had to go on. She had no choice. Zak needed her and anyway, she wanted to find out where this game went. She wasn't going to give up now.

She walked through a large hall and then up a huge, stone staircase. There were pirate pictures on the walls and she felt as if they were watching her as she went up the stairs. They gave her the creeps – a bit like that weird guy with the cone of white hair who'd been standing on the canal bridge when they found the game. She remembered with a shiver the way he'd stared and smiled. Did he have something to do with this game? Had he wanted Zak and her to find it?

She walked on. Ahead of her was a kind of gloomy corridor, lit by a few smoky candles. She gasped as she got closer. On both sides of the corridor was a line of pirates. They all had swords and stood as still as statues. They held their swords up above their heads as if they were just about to strike ... If they were just statues, then Mia didn't need to worry. But they looked so real with their mean faces and their fierce eyes that glared out of the gloom.

Mia was almost next to the first pirate now. She waited a moment. She wanted to be sure it was safe to pass between the two rows of pirates. She took a small step forward then straight away jumped back. Whoosh! All the pirates' swords chopped down together, then slowly lifted again. Mia had been right to wait. If she'd just walked down the corridor she'd have been carved up like a Christmas turkey!

Mia tried again. She stepped forward and jumped back. This time she counted the seconds while the swords were being lifted up. Nine seconds. That's how long she had to get to the end of the corridor. She had to run down the corridor *while* the pirates were lifting up their swords. Could she do it? At the end of the corridor, beyond the pirates, she could see some stairs. Mia had to climb them to reach the top of the castle and get into the tower. That's where Zak was. She had no choice. She *had* to get to the stairs to rescue Zak.

Mia shut her eyes and took a deep breath. *Come on, you can do it*, she said to herself. She was the fastest runner in her year at school so she should be OK. But this time she was running for her life.

She got herself into a good starting position. She put one leg a little in front of the other, bent her knees, got her arms ready to pump ... She was ready. One more deep breath and she took a small step forward, then back. Whoosh! The swords chopped down again. Mia waited, ready. The moment the swords started to lift, she was off. *Run, Mia, run!* she told herself.

Within seconds she was halfway to the end of the pirates. Her feet seemed to be flying. She was going to make it easily. But then disaster struck! She lost her balance and stumbled, falling to the floor. By the time she'd picked herself up, the swords were almost up above the pirates' heads. In an instant they'd chop down again. Mia had no time to think. She sprinted faster than she'd ever done before. As she reached the last pirate, she saw his sword flash in the candlelight as it started to come down. She threw herself forward, chest out, like an Olympic sprinter stretching for the finishing tape. Whoosh! She heard the swords chop down, felt something brush the back of her head. Then she fell in a heap, panting and gasping.

Mia put her hand up to her head and shivered. She felt her scalp – where the sword had cut away some of her hair. She'd been a hair's breadth away from being killed. But the important thing was that she'd reached the end of another level. How many more levels were there?

Level 7

Mia climbed the stairs. They were narrow and went round and round on their way upwards. She was puffing by the time she reached the top. Her legs hurt all over.

Ahead of her was an arch and beyond that the skull tower. There was an old pistol hanging on the wall next to the arch. *It was about time she had a weapon*, she thought. This game was full of dangers. You never knew what to expect next. Mia took the

pistol off the wall and stepped through the arch.

Now she could see the skull tower clearly. Was Zak still there? She called out his name. A few moments later she saw him in one of the skull's eye windows.

"Mia!" he shouted. "Mia, I'm trapped. I can't get out."

"It's OK, Zak!" Mia shouted back. "I'm coming to get you."

Suddenly Zak's hand shot up, pointing at something. "Look out, Mia!" he screamed.

Mia looked up. Something was flying at her. She dodged just in time and the thing passed by with an evil squawk. It looked like some kind of parrot. But she'd never heard of parrots attacking people before.

Squawk, squawk!

She turned to see another parrot. It had fierce red eyes and its beak and claws looked very sharp. This was no Pretty Polly – this was a killer pirate parrot and it was heading right at her! Mia lifted her pistol and fired.

Bang!

The parrot vanished. But there were more behind, lots of them, preparing to attack.

Mia started to run towards the tower. She forgot about how her legs hurt. She had to save Zak.

Another parrot swooped and squawked. Mia fired the pistol again, twice this time, and the bird vanished. Normally, old pistols only fired one shot and then they needed to be reloaded. Mia was glad that in this game it was different. But how many more shots *did* she have?

Mia had gone the wrong way! She wasn't at the skull tower. In front of her was a wall – nothing else. She had to turn and go back the way she had come. Two more birds swooped. Again she fired and zapped them. She tried a different way, running as fast as she could.

Two more parrots swooped at her, squawking. She shot once and the first bird vanished. She shot again, but nothing happened! The pistol just clicked. The second bird was almost on her now. She could see its mouth open as it got ready to rip its sharp beak into her. There was only one thing for it – Mia threw her pistol at the bird. It was so close she couldn't miss. The bird screeched and vanished. Mia gave a sigh. She was still alive, but now she had no weapon.

"Mia, look out! Hurry!" Zak yelled. He was pointing at something again.

Mia looked and gasped. A whole flock of parrots was getting ready to swoop. No way could she dodge all of those. She had to get to the tower before they got to her. Once again she was in a race for her life.

She sprinted towards the tower. This time, thank goodness, she'd gone the right way.

She ran up the stairs to the tower door. She reached it as the killer parrots dived at her. The noise was terrible. She rattled the iron door handle, pushed, rattled again. The door was stuck! She ducked as the first parrot swooped down at her, then pushed at the door as hard as she could. This time it swung open and she fell inside.

The door slammed shut behind her.

Level 8

"You made it, Mia, you made it!" Zak shouted. He threw his arms around his sister. She put her arms round him too. He began to cry. Mia held him tight until he could tell her what had happened to him. He had been sucked into the game like her. At first he had thought it was really cool – even when the octopus had grabbed him. He'd wriggled free quite easily and escaped into the wreck. It had been an exciting adventure. But now he'd had enough.

"I don't want to play this game any more, Mia," he sobbed. "I want to go home."

Mia hugged her little brother. "It's OK, Zak," she said softly. "This must be the last level. We'll be home soon."

"But we're locked in," Zak sobbed once more. "How can we get out?"

"We'll find a way," said Mia. "We have to."

Mia got up and went over to the door she'd come in by. It was shut tight and there was no handle on this side. She climbed into one of the eyes and looked out. It was too high up to jump out of and the walls of the tower were too smooth to climb down. She walked round the inside of the skull looking for a way out – but she couldn't see one anywhere.

Suddenly there was a red flash and a ghostly figure floated in the air in front of them.

It was a pirate with a patch over one eye and the biggest and reddest beard that Mia had ever seen. Redbeard! Of course, it was Redbeard, the Pirate King, who owned this castle. Zak grabbed Mia's hand. She could tell he was terrified. She was pretty scared herself.

"Avast and shiver me timbers!" Redbeard roared. As he spoke, the words flashed up on the walls around him. "You've made it through to the end, me hearties. Well done to yee. But it ain't quite over yet. No. There be one final test." Redbeard pointed to the floor and a puzzle with squares and letters flashed onto it. "You be inside the skull, landlubbers, and now it's time to use yer brains. Find the hidden message and you win. But be fast about it! You have but one

minute to complete yer task." He pointed at the wall and a candle lit up. "When the candle burns out, the tower will fall. Good luck and farewell!" There was another red flash and Redbeard disappeared. The candle started to burn down.

"Quick," said Mia. "We've got to solve this puzzle." She stared at the letters, then back at the candle. It was a quarter gone already. She felt sick with panic. She was hopeless at word puzzles. She'd never been good at reading or spelling. That's why she had to do extra work at home with her mum. How could she possibly do this puzzle in time? The candle was almost half gone. Half of their time had passed and they hadn't done anything!

"Mia!" Zak shouted. Mia stopped fretting about what to do. She looked down and saw Zak on the ground, moving the letters around. She thought for a moment that he was just playing around, being a pest as always.

"Zak, what are you doing?" she shouted.

He frowned up at her. "I'm doing the puzzle," he said. "I think I've almost got it."

Of course! Zak was a good reader, better than she was, even though he was younger. Thank goodness for Zak! She got down on the floor next to him.

"What can I do to help?" she asked.

"Just pass me the letters," he said. He looked up at the candle. "And fast!"

Mia worked quickly. She passed Zak the letters he wanted so that he could make the words to spell out Redbeard's message.

The candle burnt on, wax dripped. The skull tower started to shake and crack. Soon it would cave in.

The candle was three quarters gone. Only 15 seconds left. It felt to Mia like the ground was moving too. The whole tower was going to collapse.

"Quick, Zak!" she cried. "We're almost out of time!"

She passed him another letter.

The candle went down ... two words were still missing.

The candle started to flicker. Zak made another word. One more to go.

The candle's flame was dying. Mia snatched up the last letters and laid them down. Had she spelt the last word right? There was no time to change it now. She read the message –

United we stand. Divided we fall.

The candle was down to the smallest spark. The tower was shuddering and groaning. The roof was starting to fall in. This was it!

Mia threw her arms round Zak, held him tight.

The candle went out. One minute had gone! Time was up. With a terrible crash the tower collapsed. The floor split open and Zak and Mia fell through.

Level 9

Mia was lying on Zak's bed with her arms round her little brother. When, in real life, had she last done that? Zak was holding the GameBoy. His thumbs were on the controls. He was staring at the screen.

"Look," he said in a very soft voice.

Mia looked. There was a message on the screen –

"Well played! You live to fight another day. Ready to play again?"

Mia shivered. She held Zak a bit tighter.

"I don't like that game," Zak said. "I never want to play it again."

Mia shook her head. "Nor me," she agreed. "That was scary."

"It's lucky we got that message right," said Zak.

Mia nodded. *What if they hadn't?* she thought. *Where would they be now? Crushed and buried under the fallen tower?* She shivered again.

"You did really well with that puzzle," she said.

"You did really well coming to rescue me," said Zak.

Mia grinned. "We were a pretty good team, weren't we?"

"Yeah, we were," Zak grinned too.

He looked down at his feet. He only had one trainer on and they both knew where the other one was.

"Don't worry. I'll think of something to tell Mum," Mia said.

It was ages since they'd talked like this – being nice to each other, not shouting or arguing. They'd got into a pattern of getting at one another. Mia didn't know why. Maybe she should try a little harder to be nicer. Maybe Zak wasn't such a little pest after all. Well, not all the time. She thought about him in the tower with that puzzle. He'd been good.

There was a loud clanking and banging in the street outside. It was bin day. Mia sat up. She had an idea. She switched off the GameBoy. Then she took out the strange game. "Come on," she said.

Mia and Zak went downstairs and out through the front door into the street. The dustbin lorry was right outside their house now. Mia went round the back and threw the game into the lorry, among all the rubbish.

"There, that's got rid of that," she said, rubbing her hands clean.

"Good riddance," Zak added. He gave Mia a high five.

They turned back to the house. "Fancy a game of cards?" Mia asked.

"Yeah," said Zak. He grinned. "But you know I'll beat you."

"We'll see," Mia said with a laugh, and they went back inside together.

The driver of the dustbin lorry watched the two children in his mirror. He smiled and his odd eyes seemed to gleam. His cone of white hair dazzled in the sudden sunlight as he drove away down the street and then vanished.

Barrington Stoke would like to thank all its readers for commenting on the manuscript before publication and in particular:

Michelle Abbott
Harry Acfield
Megan Adeney
Reece Aherne
Kerry Anderson
Olivia Burt
David Chappell
Maria Coley
Zoe Davies
George Drysdale
Michael Entwistle
Jonathan Eustace
Jenny Gooch
Vanessa Gott
George Greenway
Natalie Greig
Luke & Emma Harrison
Joe Healey
Rory Hinton
Jacob Howard
Seb Jones
Sarah Killoh
Jack Lacey

Christine Lannigan
Sally Leszczynski
Chelsea McCallion
Hannah Meikle
Kerri Morrison
Micheál Murphy
Jamie Phelps
Maxwell Phillips
George Preece
Ellie Pryor
Kate Robinson
Conor Ross
Michael Soper
Justin Stevenson
Josie Van Es
Freddie Rochez
Jade Anthony
Alannha Balfour
Kyle Kilgour
Kevin Moffat
Hannah Walmesley-Brown
Andrew Walsh

Become a Consultant!

Would you like to give us feedback on our titles before they are published? Contact us at the email address below – we'd love to hear from you!

Email: info@barringtonstoke.co.uk
Website: www.barringtonstoke.co.uk

Great reads – no problem!

Barrington Stoke books are:

Great stories – funny, scary or exciting – and all by the best writers around!

No hassle – fast reads with no boring bits, and a brilliant story that you can't put down.

Short – the perfect size for a fast, fun read.

We use our own font and paper to make it easier for dyslexic people to read our books too. And we ask readers like you to check every book before it's published.

That way, we know for sure that every Barrington Stoke book is a great read for everyone.

Check out www.barringtonstoke.co.uk for more info about Barrington Stoke and our books!

Have you read the first Game Boy adventure?

Game Boy
by Alan Durant

JP loves computer games and he can't wait to try out his new game. But, as it starts, a strange message appears. JP finds himself in a thrilling life or death adventure and there's no going back.

Will he be good enough to make it to the end of the game?

You can order *Game Boy* directly from our website at www.barringtonstoke.co.uk